From the first Dutch edition by T. van Hoijtema
adapted and edited by Erwin Burckhardt

First published in the United States in 1964 by Atheneum.
Renewed and re-published in the United States, Great Britain, Canada, Australia, and New Zealand
in 1993 by NorthSouth Books Inc., an imprint of NordSüd Verlag AG, CH-8005 Zürich, Switzerland.
This edition first published in the United States, Great Britain, Canada, Australia, and New Zealand in
2013 by NorthSouth Books Inc., an imprint of NordSüd Verlag AG, CH-8005 Zürich, Switzerland.

Distributed in the United States by NorthSouth Books Inc., New York 10016.

Library of Congress Cataloging-in-Publication Data is available.
Printed in Germany by Grafisches Centrum Cuno GmbH & Co. KG, 39240 Calbe, January 2013.
ISBN 978-0-7358-4130-7 (trade edition)
1 3 5 7 9 • 10 8 6 4 2

www.northsouth.com

FSC
www.fsc.org
MIX
Paper from
responsible sources
FSC® C043106

Celestino Piatti
The Happy Owls

North
South

Once upon a time
in an old stone ruin
there lived a pair of owls.

All the year through
they were very happy.

On a farm nearby
there were all kinds of barnyard fowl
who did nothing all day
but eat and drink.

And after they had finished eating
and drinking, they began to fight
with one another.

They could never think of
anything better to do.

One day the peacock noticed the owls,
and he wanted to know
why they did not quarrel.

Why was it they were so happy?

When they heard his question,
the other birds said,
"Why don't you visit the owls
and ask them how they can live together
so peacefully?"

With a deep bow the peacock agreed
to call on the owls.

The peacock carefully preened
his gorgeous plumage
and strutted off in all his finery.

At the owls' house,
he spread out his tail feathers
and rustled them and clawed at the ground
to attract the owls' attention.

The owls blinked their big round eyes
when they heard what he wanted to know.

"Well, Mr. Peacock, we'll tell you,
but first go and fetch all your friends."

When the chickens, the ducks,
the geese, and all the others
were assembled,
the owls began their story.

"When spring comes, we are happy
to see everything come to life
after the long winter sleep.

"The trees put forth their buds and leaves,
the meadows are covered
with thousands of tiny flowers,
and birds everywhere are singing merrily.

"Later, around every flower,
bees and bumblebees are buzzing,
and all kinds of little flies are humming.

"Butterflies flit to and fro gathering honey
from the golden sunflowers.

"Then we know that summer is here.

"And when everything is green and growing
and the trees nod their leafy crowns to us
in the warm sunshine,
we sit in a shady nook in the cool forest
and are at peace with the world.

"Then autumn comes,
and the spider, who has waited
through the glorious summer under a leaf,
comes out and spins her web
to hold up the tired leaves a little longer.

"We rejoice to see her.

"And finally when all the leaves are fallen
and the earth is covered with snow,
we come back and are cozy in our old home—
for winter is here again."

"What nonsense!" screamed the chickens,
the ducks, the peacocks, and the geese,
for they had understood nothing of all this.

"Do you call that happiness?"

And the barnyard fowl, who preferred
to go on preening, stuffing themselves,
and quarreling, turned their backs on the owls
and went on living as before.

But the owls snuggled still closer
to each other,
blinked their big round eyes,
and went on thinking
their wise thoughts.

"You can draw an owl a thousand times, but you will never find out its secret." —Celestino Piatti

The History of the International Bestseller *The Happy Owls*

The Happy Owls is a picture book whose origins go back to the nineteenth century. In 1895 the Dutch artist Theo van Hoijtema wrote the words and drew the pictures for this fable under the title *Uilen-Geluk.* The author and translator, Erwin Burckhardt, found it fascinating, translated it into German, and suggested that Celestino Piatti should draw the illustrations for a new edition.

Piatti depicted no other subject so often and with so many variations as the owl. It became his own personal emblem and appears in all seven of his picture books. It even plays an important role in the Christmas story *The Holy Night* (1969) as a protector on the road to Bethlehem. Piatti's owls are creatures of deep significance, and they can also have different meanings. They may stand for peace, for wisdom, or for something secretive and mysterious. They are friends on whom children can always rely.

Piatti's *The Happy Owls* was first published in 1963. It was his first picture book. The story of the happy owl couple was translated into many languages and became an international best seller. The key to its success almost certainly lies in the unmistakable originality of Piatti's pictorial language. Its basis is a mixture of truth to nature and a degree of stylization. This puts the focus on whatever is essential. For instance, a special feature of the owl is its clear and penetrating gaze, which Piatti captures in masterful fashion.

"Feeling, craftsmanship and imagination were the highly concentrated ingredients of his life's work." —Bruno Weber

Celestino Piatti—Life and Work

Celestino Piatti was born in Wangen in 1922 and grew up in Dietlikon, near Zürich. He studied graphic art in Zürich from 1938 to 1942, and during this period produced his first drawings and watercolors. His very first poster (1948) won him an award and many more followed, including the Golden Brush (1976) for the book covers he designed for DTV (Deutscher Taschenbuch Verlag).
The owl motif appeared for the first time in 1952 on a poster advertising books. In addition to books and posters, Celestino Piatti designed postage stamps, stained glass, murals, ceramics, and sculptures; and he also worked as a cartoonist for the Nebelspalter. Although he used a wide variety of techniques, his style—black outlines and vivid colors—was always unmistakable. He died in 2007 in Duggingen, in the canton of Basel-Land.